Perfectly POPPY

Outside Surprise

Story by Michele Jakubowski

Pictures by Erica-Jane Waters

Picture Window Books

Perfectly Poppy is published by Picture Window Books, a Capstone Imprint
1710 Roe Crest Drive, North Mankato, MN 56003
www.capstonepub.com

Library of Congress Cataloging-in-Publication Data
Jakubowski, Michele, author.
Outside surprise / by Michele Jakubowski ; illustrated by Erica-Jane Waters.
pages cm. –– (Perfectly Poppy)
Summary: Poppy is not impressed with her best friend Millie's new playhouse, but she soon
realizes that all it needs is a little imagination to make everything work out fine.
ISBN 978-1-4795-5802-5 (hardcover) –– ISBN 978-1-4795-5806-3 (pbk.)
ISBN 978-1-4795-6204-6 (ebook)
1. Children's playhouses––Juvenile fiction 2. Imagination––Juvenile fiction. 3. Play––Juvenile
fiction. 4. Best friends––Juvenile fiction. [1. Playhouses––Fiction. 2. Imagination––Fiction.
3. Play––Fiction 4. Best friends––Fiction. 5. Friendship––Fiction.] I. Waters, Erica-Jane,
illustrator. II. Title. III. Series: Jakubowski, Michele. Perfectly Poppy
PZ7.J153555Out 2015
813.6––dc23   2014020647

Designer: Kristi Carlson

Printed in China by Nordica
0914/CA21401511
092014   008470NORDS15

Table of Contents

Chapter 1

Millie's New House 5

Chapter 2

The Little House 10

Chapter 3

Poppy's Place 16

Chapter 1

Millie's New House

On Saturday, Millie called
Poppy with some fun news. Millie
was Poppy's best friend.

"My dad is building me a
playhouse in the backyard!"
Millie said.

"That is so cool. What kind of playhouse is it?" Poppy asked.

"It's like a tree house," Millie said, "but it will be on the ground. He's been building it all day."

Poppy tried to imagine the playhouse. It would probably have big chairs, a TV, and a lot of toys. Maybe they could even have a sleepover in it!

Poppy didn't love playing
outside. But this playhouse
sounded pretty cool. In fact, it
sounded perfect!

"I'll be right over," Poppy said.

Chapter 2

The Little House

When Poppy got to Millie's
house, she raced to the backyard.
She found Millie standing in front
of a small blue house. Millie looked
really excited.

Poppy was surprised. This was
not what she thought the playhouse
would look like.

Instead of a door, a sheet hung
in the doorway. It had windows, too,
but there was no glass in them.

"Isn't it awesome?" Millie asked.

Poppy didn't know why Millie was so excited. It wasn't anything fancy at all.

"Um, yeah," Poppy said. She walked into the playhouse.

It was empty. Where were the toys and games and TV? Where were the big chairs?

"What should we play first?" Millie asked.

Poppy thought and thought.

Finally she asked, "Well, what do

you do in a playhouse?"

"That's the best part," Millie
said. "We can play whatever we
want to play! We just need to use
our imagination!"

Chapter 3

Poppy's Place

Millie and Poppy got some

snacks to help them think of

what to play. They were inside

the playhouse munching on

some crackers and cheese when

they heard a noise.

Poppy poked her head out of the front window. She saw her older brother Nolan and his friend Thomas.

"This is so cool!" Nolan said.

Just then Poppy got an idea.

"It is cool. In fact, it's a really

cool restaurant called Poppy's

Place," she said.

Millie poked her head out of a
window on the side.

"You place your order here,"
she said. "Then you go around to
the other window to pick it up."

Nolan and Thomas raced over
to Millie's window.

"Welcome to Poppy's Place!

Today's special is a burger, fries,

and a shake," Millie said.

"I'll take one," Nolan said.

Millie and Poppy pretended to be cooking the food. Poppy was having so much fun!

Then Poppy stuck her head

out the window and handed

Nolan some pretend food.

"Here you go, sir," she said

with a big smile.

The four of them took turns

being the customers and working

in the restaurant.

After that they brought out

some of Millie's stuffed animals

and played pet shop.

Nolan, Poppy, Millie, and Thomas
agreed that they would play something
different every day.

"We can play pirates!" Nolan said.

"We can bring out our dolls and play house," Millie said.

"We can even play school," Thomas said.

"That's the best thing about this playhouse," Poppy said. "With our imagination, we can play whatever we want!"

Poppy's New Words

I learned so many new words today! I made sure to write them down so I could use them again.

customer (KUSS-tuh-mur) — the person who buys things

imagination (i-maj-uh-NAY-shuhn) — ability to create ideas of things you have never experienced or are not present or real

order (OR-dur) — to ask for something

playhouse (PLAY-houss) — a small house for children to play in, usually built outside

restaurant (RESS-tuh-ruhnt) — a place where people pay to eat meals

tree house (TREE HOUSS) — a small playhouse that is built in a tree

Poppy's Ponders

I was tired after playing in the playhouse all afternoon. When I got home, I relaxed and did some thinking. Here are some of my questions and thoughts from the day.

1. I was disappointed when I saw the playhouse for the first time. Talk about a time when you were disappointed.

2. Make a list of at least five things you like to do outside.

3. If you could build your dream playhouse, what would it look like? Write a paragraph describing it. Be sure to draw a picture as well.

4. Once we started playing, I had a ton of fun ideas about what to play. If you had a playhouse, what would you play? Why?

Build Your Own Playhouse

You don't need a lot of supplies to make your own playhouse. It can be as simple or as fancy as you want. Grab boxes, pillows, blankets, sheets, or anything else that might work. Be creative!

The Card Table Cottage

Have an adult set up a card table (or other small table) for you. Grab a sheet or blanket and cover the table. If you have an old sheet, you might be able to cut out windows or draw on it. Be sure to ask permission first.

The Pillow Palace

Grab as many pillows and
blankets as you can. Stack
up the pillows and drape the
blanket over the top. (Hint: Use
couches or chairs to help keep the
blankets up.) You might want to
get a flashlight, as it might be a
little dark in your pillow palace.

The Cardboard Castle

Look around your house for
extra boxes. They can be big,
little, or medium. If you find a
big enough box (from a large
appliance), you could make your
entire playhouse out of that. If
you find lots of boxes, build up
walls as high as you can. Be sure
to grab markers and decorate
your cardboard castle!

About the Author

Raised in the Chicago suburb of Hoffman Estates, Michele Jakubowski has the teachers in her life to thank for her love of reading and writing. While writing has always been a passion for Michele, she believes it is the books she has read throughout the years, and the teachers who assigned them, that have made her the storyteller she is today. Michele lives in Powell, Ohio, with her husband, John, and their children, Jack and Mia.

About the Illustrator

Erica-Jane Waters grew up in the beautiful Northern Irish countryside, where her imagination was ignited by the local folklore and fairy tales. She now lives in Oxfordshire, England, with her young family. Erica writes and illustrates children's books and creates art for magazines, greeting cards, and various other projects.